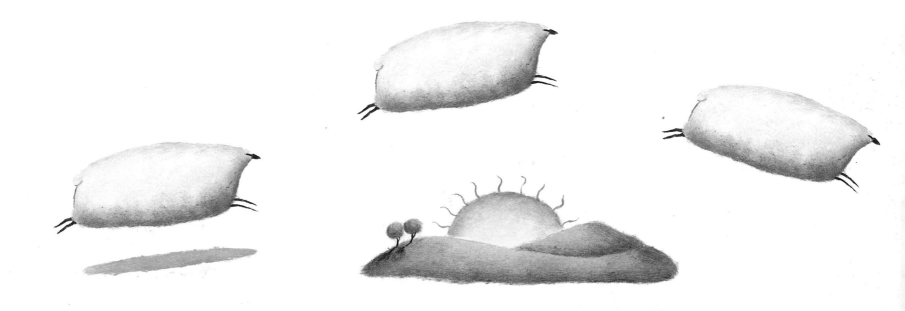

William
and the
NIGHT TRAIN

Written by
Mij Kelly

Pictures by
Alison Jay

Farrar Straus Giroux
New York

To Ma and Pa

—M.K.

To James William

—A.J.

"All aboard!" shouts the conductor. "All aboard the night train. All aboard the train that goes to Tomorrow."

teachers and jugglers, zookeepers, shopkeepers,

Mothers and fathers, sisters and brothers,

They're all sleepyheads, all ready for bed,

writers and fighters, with babies in bundles and

piglets in baskets — they all climb aboard.

all on their way to Tomorrow . . .

with wide-awake
William, who wants
to get there most
of all.

The freight car is stacked with boxes and sacks,

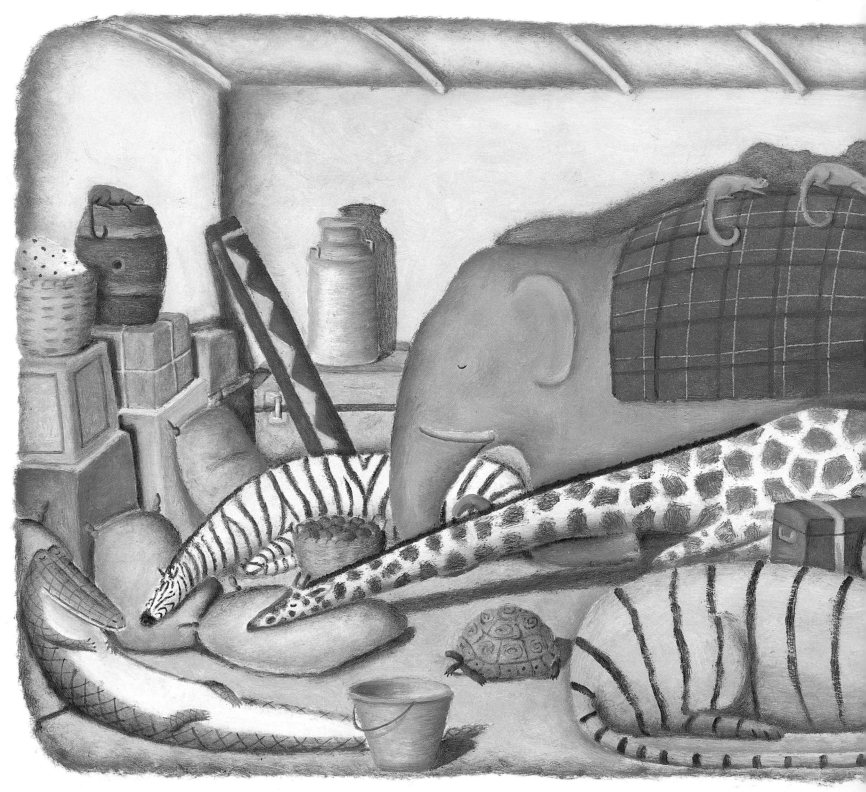

five sleepy monkeys, and a huge slumbering cat.

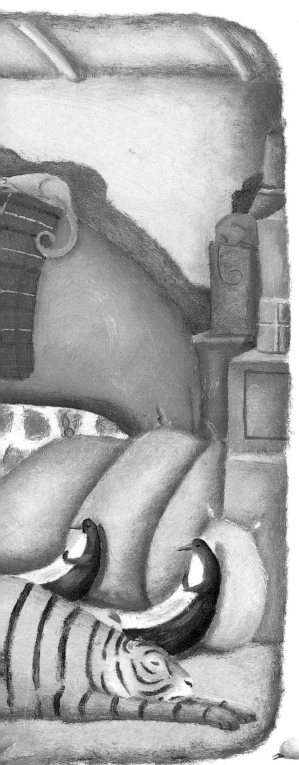

"Everyone sleeps on the night train," says William's mother. But William squirms like a worm. He wriggles. He kicks. He wants to get to Tomorrow. He wants to get there quick.

The caboose is crammed
like a box of delights with balloons and kites,

and bright
secret packages
bundled up tight.

"Everyone sleeps on the
night train," yawns the conductor.

But William's in such a giddy rush he doesn't want
to have to hush. He doesn't care if he makes a row.
He's wide awake.
He wants to get to Tomorrow NOW.

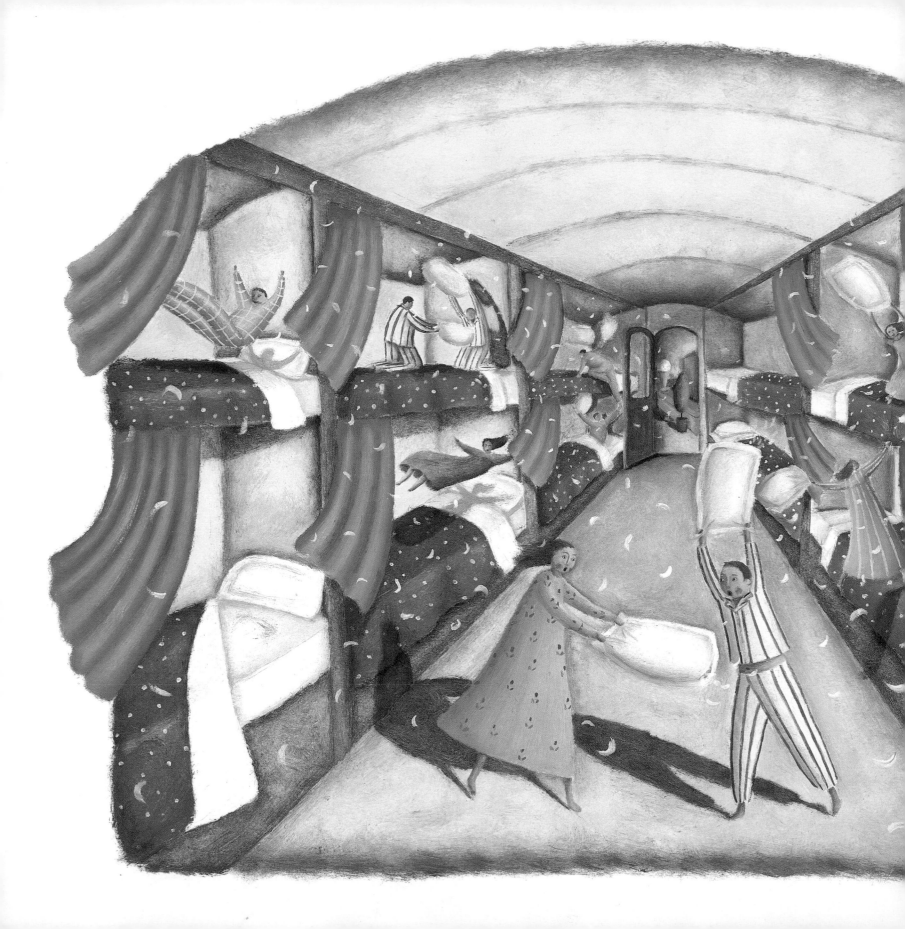

In the sleeping car, playful children bounce on their beds and hurl feather pillows at each other's heads.

"Everyone sleeps on the night train," sighs the teacher.

But William just laughs and charges on past. He whirls through the feathers; he's switched on like a light. He wants to get to Tomorrow in the middle of the night.

In the coaches, people sit nodding in rows. They slumber and doze. They're not wearing pajamas; they're still in their clothes!

"Everyone sleeps on the night train," explains the writer.

But William's too busy squishing his nose. He's too busy standing on tippity-toes. He's too wide awake. All he knows is that he can't wait for the train to go.

"When will we get to Tomorrow?"

Then his mother tells him about a trick that will make the night train go lickety-split, helter-skelter, quick as a streak.

When she cuddles him close, he can hear her heart and

a soft, sudden whoosh as the night train starts.

It pulls out of the station and into the dark,
filling the world with billows of steam,
soft see-through clouds that turn into dreams.

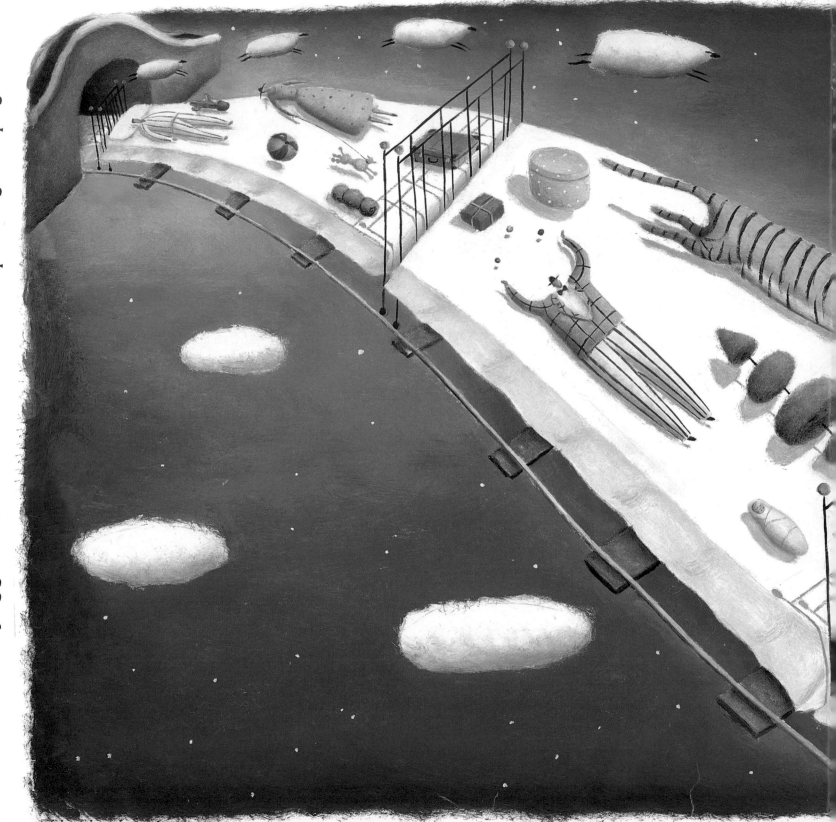

baskets and babies in bundles, brothers and mothers, and all

Teachers and jugglers, sacks, cats, and packages, piglets in

of the others speed out of today in the blink of an eye. Everyone sleeps on the night train on the way to Tomorrow . . .

even
sleepyhead
William,
who wants to
get there
most of all.